Praise for *The Singular Adventures of Rabbit and Kitty Boy*

"Kristy Deetz creates a world as it could be... as it should be, perhaps.... certainly as it exists within her vivid imagination. Her Rabbit and Kitty Boy, like *Godot*'s Vladimir and Estragon, find themselves comically confronting life's questions and realizing that there are no good answers, only more questions. A deceptive sweetness permeates her paintings, but a certain darkness around the edges of the narrative just won't leave the stories at peace. She depicts a place where myth, legend, art history and dreams come to play together, and it is a delight."

> *— Fred Stonehouse, Professor*
> *Department of Art-University of Wisconsin/Madison*

"A delightful read that acknowledges the multiplicity of human thought forms and welcomes the dreamer into The Artist's world! Writer Edward S. Louis invites us to join Rabbit and Kitty Boy as they take us through the complex and delicate visual worlds of Kristy Deetz's *Through the Veil* paintings, uncovering meaning and unpacking art history along the way."

> *— Danielle Felice Riede, Director of Graduate Program - Visual Arts*
> *Randolph H. Deer Professor in Painting*
> *Associate Professor, Herron School of Art + Design - IUPUI*

"Sit back and enjoy as a husband and wife team take you on a joyful journey with the fantastic, gentle adventures of Rabbit and Kitty Boy. You might even learn something about art and history as the story unfolds. And, not to forget, these amazing stories are accompanied by a range of beautiful images that playfully suggest the profound nature of magic realism. I felt I was transported back to another time and another world while channeling the works of Robert Louis Stevenson and Jorge Luis Borges!"

> *— Don. J. Pollack, Adjunct Associate Professor*
> *Visual Communications Design, School of the Art Institute of Chicago*

"The Singular Adventures of Rabbit and Kitty Boy is a treasure. It offers readers a world, both visual and literary, of fantasy, curiosity and discovery. One reflects on developments in the visual arts as well as the artist's creative mind through Louis' good-humored, insightful dialogue between these anthropomorphized friends. One's eyes return often to Deetz's intricately detailed, beautifully rendered paintings, the source for Louis' and our own revelations."

— Cheryl Goldsleger, Morris Eminent Scholar in Art,
Augusta University, Augusta, Georgia

"Rabbit is no ordinary rabbit. Kitty Boy is no ordinary cat. After reading just a few paragraphs of *The Singular Adventures of Rabbit and Kitty Boy*, most artists will recognize the duo as the shape-changing spirits in our heads that guide us and challenge us as we struggle with the inception and creation of each new piece of work. Like Phillip Guston, Rabbit and Kitty Boy gently remind us to acknowledge the Studio Ghosts—teachers, critics, words, theories, art histories and orthodoxies, as well as the self-doubts—that sometimes cloud our minds in the studio.

"Kristy Deetz's intriguing, smart, beautifully rendered paintings from the series, "Through the Veil" are the perfect companions for Edward S. Louis's stories, *The Singular Adventures of Rabbit and Kitty Boy*. In turn, Edward S. Louis's intelligent and humorous writing is the perfect companion for Kristy Deetz's paintings. This is a generous and joyful book: a visual feast with a healthy dose of wisdom and a welcome splash of humor that quietly tells us to trust ourselves."

— Patricia Bellan-Gillen, Dorothy L. Stubnitz Professor of Art Professor of Art
Artist & Professor Emeritus, Carnegie Mellon University

"Kristy Deetz and Edward S. Louis's collection of illustrated short stories is a Wonderland of sheer delight. The knowing and witty references to culture, art, and art criticism make the banter of Rabbit and Kitty Boy the stuff of a Tim Burton fantasy. A must-read and see for those in the know."

— Richard H. Axsom, PhD, Senior Curator Emeritus
Madison Museum of Contemporary Art

The Singular Adventures of

Rabbit and Kitty Boy

Kristy Deetz and Edward S. Louis

ELM GROVE PUBLISHING
San Antonio, Texas, USA

ISBN 978-1-943492-65-7 (hard back)
ISBN 978-1-943492-66-4 (soft cover)

ELM GROVE PUBLISHING
San Antonio, Texas, USA

www.elmgrovepublishing.com

Contents

Rabbit and Kitty Boy Escape the Postmodern Radar

"THAT DOESN'T MAKE SENSE," Rabbit said.

"What's that?" Kitty Boy asked.

"*Postmodern*," Rabbit replied. "It's either *modern*, now, or before now. If you can sit here and look at it, it can't be after now."

They were sitting together looking at a book called *Postmodern Art*.

"*Modern* in art doesn't mean *now*," Kitty Boy explained. "It means some kinds of art between the 1880s and 1950s."

"What kinds?"

"Work that rejected old ideas and tried new techniques instead, trying to get everyone to see in different ways. It prefers irony to realism."

"What's *irony*?" Rabbit asked.

"No one knows," Kitty Boy said.

9

"So postmodernism must come after modernism," Rabbit suggested.

"Exactly," Kitty Boy answered, smiling.

"What does it do?" Rabbit asked.

"It rejects old ideas and tries to make everyone see in new ways."

"That's what you said about modernism," Rabbit said doubtfully.

"It brings into question everything we think we know. It casts a radar over art, language, science, poetry—everything—to see what lies behind it." Kitty Boy was doing his best to explain.

"Radar," Rabbit mumbled— "that sounds scary."

"I know," Kitty Boy said. "Hey, I have an idea: let's go flying! We can look around to see if we can spot the radar to see what it's looking for."

"Great idea," Rabbit said. "But I don't want just to see the radar. I want to get free of it, so it's not following us around all the time trying to ruin our ideas. Hop on! Say, you're looking very Victorian today." He admired Kitty Boy's outfit.

"Thank you," Kitty Boy said.

Kitty Boy jumped on Rabbit's back, and off they went.

"Where to?" Rabbit asked.

"Higher!" Kitty Boy said. "This sky's looking awfully *Georgia O'Keeffe* to me."

"Okay?" Rabbit asked, as they went higher.

"Higher still!" Kitty Boy exclaimed. "Look there's a butterfly. Let's go talk to him. Hey, he kind of looks like you."

"Like *me*?" Rabbit asked.

"Hello," the butterfly said, surprised to see someone flying so near.

"Hello," Kitty Boy said. "We're trying to escape the postmodern radar. Do you have any idea how to do it?"

"Why do you want to do that?" the butterfly asked.

"We don't want it to catch us and ruin our ideas," Rabbit answered.

"Well, there it is, down below," the butterfly said. "Look: you've already flown above it."

Rabbit and Kitty Boy looked down, and there they saw the radar. They had indeed escaped it, at least for a little bit.

"I feel better already," Rabbit said.

"Me, too," Kitty Boy replied. "Thank you, butterfly."

"Don't mention it."

"What are you thinking about now that we're free to think whatever we want?" Kitty Boy asked.

"Not much of anything," Rabbit said. "How about you?"

"Me either. But I like being up here. Maybe we can just fly around for a bit, and something will come to us."

"Good idea," Rabbit said. And they did.

Where's Kitty Boy?

"I HAD A VERY STRANGE DREAM," Rabbit said.

"Tell me about it," Kitty Boy suggested.

They were sitting together in the sun, and Rabbit was nibbling on a sweet piece of grass.

"It felt like a Zen dream, except not happy."

"Not everything in life goes happily."

"I know," Rabbit said. But some things seem scarier than others."

"That's true," Kitty Boy said. "Do you remember the end of the dream? Maybe if it has a good ending, you'll feel better about the rest."

"How about if I start at the beginning?"

"That's all right, too. Go right ahead," Kitty Boy said.

"I was striding along in a landscape that looked like a Chinese painting," Rabbit said, "except I wasn't entirely myself. I had long legs that looked and felt like carrots."

"Carrots! Hmmm . . . I know what they look like, but what does a carrot feel like?"

"Stiff, kind of like walking on stilts."

"I've never done that," Kitty Boy said. "What does that feel like?"

"Stiff and wobbly: you're way up off the ground standing on tall posts, and you walk by raising and pushing along the posts. You feel like you could fall at any time, but you just have to keep walking, because you don't know any way to get down from the posts."

"That does sound scary. Maybe you could walk over to a tree, step off the stilts onto a branch, and climb down the trunk," Kitty Boy offered.

"I like that idea. I'll try it if I ever again find myself on stilts made of carrots in a dream. But that wasn't why I felt scared."

"Why, then?"

"Because I was looking all over and couldn't find you!" Rabbit exclaimed. "I thought you were lost, and I was striding and striding everywhere looking for you."

"Thank you."

"No need to thank me. Just don't get lost again."

"I wasn't really lost. You were dreaming."

"It sure felt real at the time, so don't get lost even when I'm dreaming."

"Maybe I can help you find me."

"Do you think so?" Rabbit found that idea helpful.

"Yes—just let me think for a moment. You're walking through a Chinese landscape painting looking for me. Where would I be? Ah, I know: fishing!"

"Fishing!"

"Yes, I'm sitting meditatively by a stream and fishing."

"Why would you do that?"

"Because I'm hungry."

"You're always hungry."

"I'll share my fish with you, if you'd like some."

"How can I share your fish when I can't even find you?"

"I'm right by the stream, dressed in a robe, at the bottom of the painting. Look."

"Hey, how did you do that? All you had to do was say it, and there you are in my dream, true as life."

"That's the nice thing about dreams: they can come true. But be careful."

"Why?" Rabbit asked.

"Because some dreams can become nightmares," Kitty Boy warned. "Make sure you're having a good dream before you let it come true."

"If it's a dream, I'm not sure I can control it so easily," Rabbit said.

"I'm hungry," Kitty Boy said.

"Yes, I know: you're hungry in the dream, and that's why you're fishing."

"No," Kitty Boy said. "I mean I'm hungry really, now. Want to go get something to eat?"

"I could eat," Rabbit answered. "Maybe not carrots today, though."

"Maybe in another dream you could walk on fish," Kitty Boy said. He was full of suggestions that day.

"Walking on fish? That doesn't make any sense. Fish can't live out of water. And I'd probably slip right off of them and fall."

"Dreams don't always make sense," Kitty Boy said. "Sometimes they just happen."

"Kind of like art," Rabbit concluded.

Rabbit and Kitty Boy Mend the Fabric of Meaning

"I've been worried about something," Kitty Boy said.

"What's that?" Rabbit asked.

"Ever since we talked about postmodernism, I've been worried about the fabric of meaning. If nothing means anything for sure, then won't everything, the whole nature of being, tear apart?"

Rabbit looked away, and when he turned back toward Kitty Boy, he said in his best James Dean imitation, "You're tearing me apart!"

"Sorry," Kitty Boy replied sheepishly, "but I've been thinking about it a lot. Shouldn't we do something?"

"What can we do?"

"I'm not sure. Right now, I have no idea."

"Let me ask you something," Rabbit said. "Why is it the *fabric* of meaning? What does fabric have to do with anything except, well, *fabric*?"

"That's just an expression."

"An expression of what?"

"You know," Kitty Boy explained, "a metaphor. The fabric of meaning is the whole idea of meaning, all of it woven together. The whole of our understanding of the world."

"I never have understood metaphors," Rabbit said. "And as for meaning: what does *meaning* mean, anyway?"

Kitty Boy thought for a moment. "That one's too hard for me."

They sat quietly for a bit.

"I have an idea," Rabbit said.

"Tell me!"

"Let's go adventuring. We'll run a little and fly a little and see if we can find the fabric of meaning. It'll be fun if you don't worry too much."

"Great idea! Let me get a couple things, and we'll go."

Kitty Boy came back in just a minute dressed for flying. "Are you ready?" he asked?

"Hop on," Rabbit said. "We'll be just like St. George and the dragon."

"Good for you," Kitty Boy said. "A metaphor."

Off they flew through green landscapes and brown landscapes and white landscapes and finally blue and purple landscapes that looked like Persian miniatures. Rabbit was getting tired, so they dropped gently toward the ground.

"Look!" Kitty Boy said. "Right there!"

"Right there what?" Rabbit asked, panting.

"A tear in the fabric of meaning. I see one! Let's fix it!"

"How can we do that?"

"Look what I brought along. Can you fly over by it?"

"Oh, yes, I see it now! Here we go, but let's just walk the rest of the way."

"High-ho, Silver!" Kitty Boy called out, and he pulled out the needle and thread he'd put in the pocket of his coat."

"Good thinking," Rabbit said. "You brought just the right things."

"Who knows how many more of these tears we'll find out there," Kitty Boy mused.

Rabbit wasn't too happy when he heard the word *many*.

"Let's just start with this one. I'm tired. Maybe then we can go home and have supper."

"Supper, yes. I see what you mean. The fabric will still be here in the morning."

"My thoughts exactly," Rabbit said.

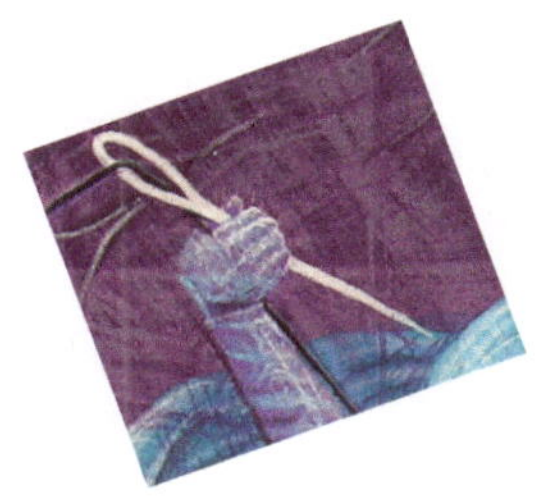

Both Sides Now

"IMAGINE WHAT IT WOULD BE LIKE to be a dinosaur," Rabbit suggested.

Rain had been falling all day, and he and Kitty Boy had been trying to think of something interesting to do.

"Why would I want to do that?" Kitty Boy asked, but he was really glad that Rabbit was wondering about something.

"Just for fun," Rabbit replied. "Think about it. If you were a Tyrannosaurus Rex, you could bite the head off of almost any other dinosaur out there, except maybe a Triceratops."

"Why would I want to do that?"

"Better than mice: much more filling. Better than birds: people always stop you from trying to eat those."

Kitty Boy remembered when someone had tried to put a bell around his neck to warn any birds about his approach. Kitty Boy could be swift on his feet, like Rabbit, and he had to admit that he liked sitting by the window and calling to the birds to get them to come closer. He licked his lips at the thought, though of course he'd never actually eaten one. He had, though, scrambled and contorted until he'd got free of that bell. But the memory still haunted him. Mostly he remembered a big, pink face with a wide, toothy smile that looked friendlier than it really was and lots of hands that moved very quickly. Those hands had left the bell, and the smile stuck around for a while after, until he'd got the bell safely off. Then the smile had disappeared, too.

He also remembered a time when someone, thinking it would look nice, had put a collar with a bow around his neck. Terrible ideas, he thought, and shivered.

"Why are you shivering?" Rabbit asked. "Rain getting to you?"

"No. I was just remembering something. I don't think I'd want to live in a place with dinosaurs around."

"Why not?"

"I think they wouldn't just eat each other. They'd try to eat us, too."

"Do you think so? That's a horrible idea!" Rabbit imagined a dinosaur dashing by, then turning to look at him out of the corner of its hungry eye.

"Some of them could fly, too," Kitty Boy added.

"Fly! Really? I had no idea!"

"Well, you were just imagining," Kitty Boy said consolingly, "so no harm done. We don't have any dinosaurs now."

"Are you sure?" Rabbit asked.

"No, not sure."

"Pretty sure?"

"Yes, pretty sure."

"Phew."

Kitty Boy was thinking about how imagination can get dangerous sometimes. Then he added, "But we have other scary things."

"Like what?"

"Well, bells and bows, for instance."

"Bells and bows! They're just decorations! Why would they be scary?"

"Depends on who's using them and for what."

"Rabbit thought for a minute. He imagined Kitty Boy wearing a bell and bow and thought he might look splendid that way. Then he imagined himself wearing a bell and a bow, and he shivered.

"Rain getting to you?" Kitty Boy asked.

"No," Rabbit said, "just imagining something."

"What?"

"Nothing interesting. Hey, look: I think the sun's going to come out."

"Look at that cloud passing by. I wonder what kind it is."

"I really don't know clouds at all," Rabbit mused, trying not to think about bells.

Somnambulists

"I THOUGHT I WAS AWAKE, BUT MAYBE I'M SLEEPING," Kitty Boy said.

"Why do you think so?" Rabbit asked.

"Because I'm seeing some strange images."

"Hmmmm . . . Do they look a little bit like us, but kind of wobbly and wavy and in strange colors, almost fading out of view?"

"Yes. Hey!" Kitty Boy exclaimed. "We're both asleep . . ."

"And we're having the same dream!" they said together.

"What an odd thing," Rabbit said.

"Maybe not," Kitty Boy said. "Maybe it happens all the time, but nobody talks about it."

"I'm wondering about the dog who's standing there with us, on the right: who's that?"

"Not sure. Maybe it's Offissa Pupp."

"You're full of *maybes* today," Rabbit observed.

"Maybe," Kitty Boy replied.

"I don't think it can be Offissa Pupp."

"Why not?"

"Well, first of all he's probably copyrighted, and second, you're not Krazy, and third, if he is the Offissa, where's Ignatz? Hey, you haven't eaten the mouse, have you?"

Kitty Boy sniffed superciliously. "I haven't eaten a mouse in a very long time, and I have no intention to do so."

"But you might do in a 'dream' what you wouldn't do in 'waking life.'"

"Hmmmm . . . Maybe. Now that I look at him more closely, he doesn't look like the Offissa anyway. He looks more like us. Do you have a friend who's a dog?"

"I've traveled a lot and had lots of adventures and made lots of friends. But maybe he's a friend of yours."

"I don't think so." Kitty Boy thought about the dog next door, Bo-Doggy, but he hadn't met him yet. Maybe just knowing about someone was enough to have him show up in your dream. "You know what? I think The Artist painted him in. Either that or the dog is having the dream along with us right now."

"That's a creepy thought: someone we don't know barging into our dream," Rabbit said.

"He doesn't seem to be causing any trouble, though. Maybe we're part of The Artist's dream, and she's dreaming the painting—or dreaming us dreaming the painting."

"I wonder what The Artist will call the painting," Rabbit said.

"I think she'll call it *Somnambulists*."

"What does that mean?"

"It means sleep-walkers," Kitty Boy explained.

"Then why doesn't she just call it that?"

"Don't know. Maybe you should ask her."

"Maybe I will."

"Or I can ask. I think I'm waking up now."
"Me, too. I think so. Except that's one odd-looking moon."

Do You Hear What I Hear?

"How about we do something different today," Rabbit suggested.

"Okay," Kitty Boy answered amenably. "What would you like to do?"

"Today you fly, and I'll ride."

"Well, that seems more than fair, but I haven't learned how to fly yet," Kitty Boy said sadly. "I'm sorry."

"Hmmm," Rabbit muttered, thinking. "Ah, I have it! You *run*, and I'll ride!"

"That sounds fine! Hop on when you're ready, and we'll go adventuring."

Kitty Boy puffed himself up to look as much as he could like a lion, and Rabbit decided to take the shape of Durga-Shakti.

"I need a sword so I can look splendid," Rabbit said.

"I don't have one," Kitty Boy said. "You'll just have to imagine it— you're always good at that."

"You're right: I'll imagine a green one to match the landscape. Matching accessories always make a good impression. I'm ready. On, Scout!"

"Together we look invincible," Kitty Boy said proudly. "Where shall we go?"

"Wherever you'd like. There's a nice, green landscape ahead with lots of wonderful draperies decorating it and clouds bigger than trees. I've been there before, and you can never tell who may meet you or what you'll hear."

Kitty Boy gave his best lion roar, and off they dashed at a tremendous pace, diving over fields and mountains and lakes and a bayou or two and some condo complexes until they saw someone lurking ahead. Though Kitty Boy couldn't figure out how to fly, he liked to show Rabbit or anyone else how fast he could run.

"Someone's lurking ahead," Rabbit warned. He looked around and found that they had come to a strange land indeed.

"I'll slow down, and we'll talk to them."

"Who are they?" Rabbit wondered. "Could they be the three kings from the Christmas song?"

"They look more like nuns to me," Kitty Boy answered. "Or they could be three rabbits. I can't tell from here. Let's get closer, and we'll ask." He was eager to make some new friends.

When Kitty Boy began to offer a greeting, he'd forgotten that he'd turned himself into a lion, and instead of his usual genteel voice with only the slightest posh accent, out came an enormous roar, and his casual smile had become a menacing grimace. To try to look friendlier, Rabbit offered them a lotus flower, but he didn't realize that his eyes had turned a burning red color. Like Kitty Boy, he had got caught up in the moment. Rabbit and Kitty Boy didn't often have

Religious orders visit them, so they weren't sure just what to do.

Sometimes you can look scary without even trying.

Hearing the roar, the three figures spoke to one another, and then they bowed. But they said nothing to the unusual-looking pair before them. The oddest thing to Kitty Boy was that sometimes they seemed to be changing into nuns, and sometimes they seemed to be changing into rabbits. Rabbit noticed that one had a little flame flickering above her head, as though she were having a wonderful idea, and he wondered what it was.

Rabbit and Kitty Boy tried to speak to them in every language they could think of, and Kitty Boy tried especially hard not to roar again.

Every now and then the three figures would bow, but finally, without saying anything, they turned and went away.

"I think we scared them," Rabbit said. "Maybe we should have remained who we are instead of becoming a lion and Durga."

"Do you know who they were?"

"No idea, and hardly a clue."

"It's like the story of Chuang-tse," Kitty Boy suggested.

"I don't remember it."

"Chuang-tse dreamed he was a butterfly, dancing in the breeze, until he awoke to find himself a man. But later Chuang-tse couldn't determine whether as a man he had dreamed he was a butterfly, or as a butterfly he dreamed he was a man."

"Subtle, but interesting," Rabbit mused.

"Let's go home," Kitty Boy said. "I'm getting hungry." He turned and roared, and off they went, Rabbit's eyes gleaming.

Devouring and Reconstructing Kali

Rabbit and Kitty Boy were sitting in the sunshine.

Kitty Boy was doing one of his favorite things: watching a butterfly flutter by. He was wondering if it might be Chuang-tse.

"I had a strange dream last night," Rabbit said.

"Oh?" He wondered if Rabbit had also dreamed about their adventure with the rabbit-nuns, since he certainly had.

"I've been thinking a lot about it. It would make a good painting. I'm calling it *Devouring and Reconstructing Kali*."

Hearing Rabbit's title, Kitty Boy swiped his paw up and tried to catch the butterfly. He was thinking Chuang-tse might be good to have around if Rabbit was going to talk about his dreams, which inevitably required difficult interpretation.

"That's ambiguous," Kitty Boy observed, since he had missed the butterfly, and it had fluttered off. "It could mean that Kali is the one who does the devouring and reconstructing, or it could mean that someone else is devouring and reconstructing Kali. Which one does it mean?"

"The second one would be dangerous," Rabbit said, "since in all the stories Kali is very powerful."

"What does she do?"

"She dances on Shiva, who is pretty powerful himself, and sometimes she destroys creatures, and sometimes she protects them."

"How do you know which one she will do?" Kitty Boy asked.

"I guess you try to be good so that she will protect you and not destroy you. They also say she liberates the sorrowful and the dead."

"Either way, it will all happen in the fullness of time."

"A wise thought," Rabbit admitted.

"What else happens in the dream?" Kitty Boy asked.

"I'm not sure I want to talk about it," Rabbit replied.

Kitty Boy knew that when Rabbit says he doesn't want to talk about something, he wants to talk about it, and all you have to do is wait.

"I dreamed that I was out by myself at night under the moon, and I had thrown a rope around a mountain and was going to pull it down."

"Why would you do that?"

"I don't know. It seemed like a good idea at the time. A flower with a face in it stood on the top of the mountain, and a white rooster was falling from the sky."

"You've told me about many of your dreams," Kitty Boy said, "but this one is as strange as any of them. What happened next?"

"The sword of Kali appeared and cut me in half." Rabbit shivered. "I guess I should have left the flower alone."

"Oh, that's terrifying!"

"Yes, but another strange thing happened. Part of me fell away, a ghost, cut in half. But part of me stayed right there. I still had the rope, ready to pull down the mountain, but I didn't want to do it anymore. It seemed silly rather than interesting."

"Did you still feel afraid?"

"That's maybe the strangest part of all. I didn't feel afraid anymore. I felt better. Kali had cut away part of me that I didn't really want to be."

"Do you still feel better now?"

"Yes, I think so."

"What happened to the chicken?"

"Chicken? Oh, the rooster—I don't know."

"Maybe we should go back to your dream and look for it."

"Why? Are you getting hungry."

"We should go home for lunch."

"It will all happen in the fullness of time."

See Brown

"I HAD ANOTHER ONE OF THOSE DREAMS," Rabbit said.

"Another nightmare?" Kitty Boy asked.

"Yes."

"Do you want to talk about it."

"No."

"Okay."

They had both eaten breakfast and were sitting on soft cushions digesting. Kitty Boy was lying back and twirling a bright yellow flower between his paws.

"I had become a chocolate rabbit, and I was melting" Rabbit said.

"In the dream?"

"Yes. The landscape had gotten terribly hot. A tall thermometer with a silly face had a bulb full of bright red blood that was about to burst. In the background a fire was raging, and bodies and other strange shapes were flying every which way! The flames were spreading, and they burned so hot that they were melting me into a sea of chocolate."

"You don't have to worry. You're not a chocolate rabbit. In real life you could run away."

"Have you ever seen *Bambi*?" Rabbit asked.

"The movie? No."

"Mm-hmm." Rabbit was surprised that Kitty Boy had never seen it, since they both loved movies, but he thought he shouldn't say any more about it. He began to think about abstract expressionism.

"Did you see anything hopeful in the dream?" Kitty Boy asked.

"Funny, but I did," Rabbit replied.

"What was that?" Rabbit liked to have Kitty Boy encourage him, and Kitty Boy knew it.

"Right in the front of the landscape, not far from where I stood, I saw a bright pink lotus flower growing out of lively green leaves."

"That certainly seems hopeful to me. What do you think it means?"

"The flower?"

"Yes."

"I don't know."

Kitty Boy liked interpreting. He played with the flower as he thought about it. "It was a dream, right? And dreams are always full of symbols. I think the chocolate rabbit wasn't you at all. I think you were the flower."

"Really? That's interesting. Why do you think so?"

"Think about it. A chocolate rabbit isn't alive. It just sits there still as can be until someone eats it! The one in your dream was melting: that's an old part of you that you don't need anymore, that you've left behind. It's melting away. The world is melting it away, so it won't bother you and keep you from new adventures. You're not the rabbit; you're the flower. The flower is bright and changing and growing and alive, like you. Here." Kitty Boy handed Rabbit his flower.

"But this flower will die. You picked it already, and it will decay and die."

Rabbit was impressed that Kitty Boy could make a speech with both a colon and a semicolon used correctly, but he felt a little worried about the dead flower.

"I didn't pick it. It fell from the plant, and the plant has lots more, just like adventures. Let's go out and find another one. We won't pick it. We'll just sit there and admire it as it grows on the plant."

"Okay," Rabbit said. The idea encouraged him.

"New flowers always grow. Think about the new flower before you sleep, my friend, and maybe you won't have nightmares."

"I'll try it!" Rabbit said, feeling hopeful again.

He noticed, though, that the day was growing warm already.

[9]

In Front of Piero's Resurrection

"I THINK I'M DOING BETTER with my nightmares," Rabbit said.

They were strolling in the garden, and Kitty Boy was looking at a cloud that might have come right out of a Luca Signorelli painting. He thought he saw a familiar face in it. One of his favorite hobbies was watching clouds to see what they looked like. But then he wondered what Rabbit had done to get control over his dreams.

"I'm glad," he said. "Tell me about it!"

They settled onto a nice spot of soft grass, and Rabbit began to explain.

"In my dream last night, I was being attacked by an enormous snake."

"Snake! That doesn't sound any better!"

"Not at first. The snake was really scary. But then I began to think about the situation, and I decided I should change how I approached it."

"Wow, that's impressive. Please go on." Kitty Boy wanted to take another look at that cloud, but he stopped himself and fixed his attention on his friend.

"Instead of feeling soft and vulnerable, I decided to feel strong, lean, and in charge of the situation."

"You must have been wearing your red tie. You always feel more confident when you wear that tie."

"You're right: I was. I was also carrying a top hat—a *magic* top hat."

"Where did you get that?"

"No idea," Rabbit replied. "You know how things go in dreams. Sometimes you just think of something, and there it is."

"What made you think of a magic top hat?"

"I guess I needed an advantage, and the top hat came to mind. Once I had that, I felt like I had a secret that could overwhelm the snake."

Kitty Boy wasn't sure how even a *magic* top hat could give Rabbit an advantage against a giant snake, but he realized Rabbit was right, that dreams seldom make any sense, and you just have to go with the flow.

"So the snake had encircled me, and it had opened its mouth wide to swallow me . . ."

"Yikes!"

"And I turned and looked it right in the eye, because I knew something that it didn't know, and I had an idea that would defeat the snake utterly."

"Tell me! I can't wait."

"I was going to pull you out of the hat and throw you at him!"

"Me? Why would you do that?" Kitty Boy couldn't believe that Rabbit would pull him out of a hat and throw him at a giant snake. That didn't seem like something one friend should do with another.

"You were going to come out of the hat in the shape of a huge lion, like the time we met the nuns, and you were going to roar and shake the world and scare him off!"

Kitty Boy felt a little better about that. He was glad that Rabbit had enough confidence in him to believe he could roar like a lion and shake the whole world and scare off a giant snake. He tried to make a huge roar, and it came out "MMMmmeeeoOOOW!"

"That's pretty good," Rabbit said. "I knew you could do it. That's why I was ready to stare down that nasty snake."

I hope you never have to, Kitty Boy thought, not sure that even a pretty good roar would be enough.

"I saw another odd thing," Rabbit recalled. "A little bit of blood, as if the snake had bitten me. But it hadn't. The blood came from something in the landscape behind me, something really powerful."

"Maybe that's what scared the snake, not my roar at all," Kitty Boy muttered.

"Could be. But whatever it was, I feel like a new rabbit today, kind of reborn."

"Wonderful! Let's go back inside and celebrate with a snack." No snakes in there, giant or otherwise, Kitty Boy thought.

"An excellent idea."

As they went back to the house, Kitty Boy looked up in sky to see if the cloud was still there, but it had gone. The sky looked clear and blue as could be. Clear is good, he thought, but he'd have liked another look at that cloud.

Glad You're Here!

Rabbit and Kitty Boy were sitting on the fence. A large, sunny field spread out before them. Rabbit was looking to see who was playing out there, but Kitty Boy had something on his mind.

"Now you've got me doing it," Kitty Boy sighed.

"Doing what?" Rabbit asked.

"Having nightmares."

"Oh, no! How did I do that?"

"By telling me about yours all the time. I think about yours, and now I have my own."

"What did you dream about?"

Kitty Boy knew that in the reverse situation Rabbit would say, "I don't want to talk about it," but he decided *he* wanted to talk about it.

"Okay, so you're out in this big landscape with bright green grass and quirky purple mountains and pointy orange creatures circling around you and bright yellow kitschy Easter bunnies with silly grins and little blue plants and creatures that look like little rabbits drawn by small children, and you're standing there wearing a red sweater and you're looking at me and smiling as you're about ready to take a picture of me with an antique camera set on a tripod. . . ." Kitty Boy paused for breath.

"Well that all seems pretty good—nothing nightmarish so far. I'd be glad to take your picture, especially with that splendid hat you're wearing today."

"Then something goes terribly wrong."

"What could go wrong?" Rabbit asked.

"You're not going to like it."

"Tell me anyway."

"A bomb is about to drop on you." Kitty Boy whispered.

"A what?"

"A bomb! You know those awful things that people toss at one another when they want to blow them to bits."

"Can they do that? Do they?"

"Yes, I'm sorry to say they do. I worry about it sometimes."

"I'm sorry to hear about that. I had no idea."

Kitty Boy was beginning to think he shouldn't have told his friend about the dream. He didn't mention that he thought the landscape in his dream may have been bombed many times before.

Rabbit thought for a moment, and he said, "But even if they throw bombs on one another, why would they want to throw one on me?"

"Sometimes they just throw them on everybody indiscriminately."

Rabbit was pretty sure he knew the meaning of *indiscriminately*. Then another idea struck him.

"Wait a minute. You were having the dream. Maybe the people didn't throw the bomb: maybe *you* threw it on me!"

"I couldn't have done it: I was standing there in my new hat waiting for you to take my picture."

"Oh, that's right. But maybe it was—what do you call it? —one of those *Freudian* things. You want it to happen, so you dream about it."

Rabbit was getting worried.

"You're my best friend," Kitty Boy assured him. "I wouldn't ever do that to you!"

"I'm glad to hear it," Rabbit said, but he sniffed with just a hint of offense.

"Please don't be offended," Kitty Boy said. "As I think about it, last night one of the people was watching a tv show about war. Bombs were dropping all over the place, making a terrible mess."

"What's *war*?" Rabbit asked.

"That's when lots and lots of people throw bombs all over the place, making a terrible mess."

"What an awful idea. Why would they do something like that?"

Kitty Boy thought about that for a long time, long enough that Rabbit suspected he'd forgotten the question. Finally, he said, "I don't know. I just don't know."

Rabbit figured that if Kitty Boy didn't know, probably not much of anyone would.

"Let's go into the field to see who's out to play," Kitty Boy said.

"Yes, let's." Rabbit jumped down off the fence thinking that Kitty Boy'd had a really odd dream. But as he hopped toward the field, he couldn't help but look up, wanting to make sure there weren't any bombs. He decided to stop worrying and love the day.

Playing Chess with Duchamp

RABBIT HAD TAKEN UP PAINTING, and one pleasant morning Kitty Boy found him out in the back yard working busily with a brush, a palette full of colors, and a canvas. He was wearing a stylish French beret and a dashing white silk scarf, which he'd thrown back over his shoulder so he could paint without its getting in his way.

"So you're really serious about painting," Kitty Boy said, having waited for Rabbit to pause so he wouldn't interrupt the creative process.

"Ah, there you are!" Rabbit said. "I've been waiting for you. Here: I got these for you." He took off the beret and scarf and held them out to Kitty Boy.

"For me? What a lovely gift. But you look so suave in them! You should keep them for yourself."

"Not as suave as you," Rabbit said. "You're the one who knows how to wear clothes." He put the cap on Kitty Boy's head and draped the scarf around his neck. "There: now you look really stylish. We could go on an adventure, and everyone would admire you."

"Thank you!" Kitty Boy said. "What are you painting?" He rubbed the silk scarf between his paws pleasurably.

"Come see."

"Oh, here, I almost forgot: I brought a nice fresh carrot for you."

"Thank you. Just what I needed: I was ready for a break."

Kitty Boy walked around and looked at the canvas as Rabbit munched eagerly on his carrot.

"You're making a painting of your favorite person. And she's painting."

"Yes, the painter: she's painting a picture of me painting. What do you think?"

Kitty Boy was thoroughly impressed. "Marvelous. You've captured her perfectly."

"Well, she is my favorite person, so I wanted to do her justice."

"What inspired you?" Kitty Boy asked.

"I saw her in her studio painting. She was painting a picture of me painting."

"I hope she does you justice, too. Hey, I have an idea: let's go see!"

"Right!" Rabbit said.

They went back of the house where Rabbit's favorite person, The Artist, had her painting studio. They hopped up on the window sill and looked in.

There sat The Artist at her easel. She was just finishing her painting of Rabbit, and she had indeed captured his character, his style and verve, perfectly.

"She's amazing," Kitty Boy said. "Her painting is almost as good as yours."

"Do you think so?"

"See how energetic you look. You're painting an Easter egg with parrots and flowers on it, and it's flowing back into the landscape. Everything in the painting bursts with activity. Look at the background: it's a chess board with another painting behind it, this one by Duchamp."

"Hmmm . . . My painting has a checkerboard: I like checkers better than chess. By the way, who's Duchamp?"

"A famous painter."

"You do know your painters."

"And now I know the one who will be most famous of all."

"Who's that?" Rabbit asked.

"Why, you, of course!"

Rabbit blushed. He felt thoroughly repaid for the cap and scarf.

"I wonder why she painted me painting an Easter egg rather than painting a picture of her," Rabbit mused.

"Infinite regression," Kitty Boy said, "it has to stop somewhere."

"Infinite what?"

"A painter painting a painting of a painter painting a painting of a painter . . ."

"Got it," Rabbit said. "What a fun game. Well, time to get back to work. You don't have any more of those carrots, do you?"

"I'll get you some," Kitty Boy said. He adjusted his beret to the perfect rakish angle, tightened his new scarf, and dashed back to the garden for more carrots.

[12]

Through Darger's Eyes

"Is that supposed to be you?" Kitty Boy asked. He and Rabbit were back up on the window sill of the painting studio looking in. The Artist was just finishing another new painting.

"She certainly is productive," Rabbit said. He worked more slowly, so he admired how The Artist could do so many wonderful paintings so quickly.

He didn't realize that the painter labored for many months over every painting and that she wished she could work more quickly. Of course, she knew she couldn't work any faster and still attend to the level of detail that she wanted. But that's a different story.

"Does that look like me: the rabbit in the painting?" Rabbit asked.

"Nooooo," Kitty Boy answered, drawing out the syllable. "Do you know for sure if it's supposed to look like you?"

"No, I don't. I guess I shouldn't assume that every rabbit she paints should represent me." He was feeling just a little hurt. "What *do* I look like?" Rabbit asked.

"Oh: you look like you, like *Rabbit,* my best friend. No one could mistake you for someone else. Hmmm, don't you know what you look like?"

"No. How would I know that?"

"Haven't you ever looked down into the stream at the back of the field?"

"Yes, but I saw only some wavy lines with a fuzzy shape behind them. Have you looked in? Did you see me there?"

"I've looked in—you have to wait a moment until the water is still and your eyes adjust—but all I saw was a very handsome cat wearing a nifty beret." Kitty Boy smiled.

"A beret—like yours? My, that is a coincidence."

Kitty Boy thought he might explain the joke, but then decided not to.

"Come on," Kitty Boy said. "Let's go out to the stream and I'll show you." They jumped down to the yard, dashed toward the fence, and leaped over. The grass was getting high in the old field, and they lost each other a couple times on the way, but finally they made it to the stream.

"Who's *Darger*?" Rabbit asked.

"Henry Darger? He was a reclusive American artist who made an enormous book, *The Story of the Vivian Girls,* full of watercolor paintings. Why do you ask?"

"I saw his name on a paper on the wall next to the painting. The Artist usually writes down her titles there."

"You have a sharp eye," Kitty Boy said.

"And once again you amaze me with your knowledge of painters.

How did you learn so much?"

"From her books. When she's not looking, I read them—but mostly I look at the pictures. One thing I can tell you: she's as good an artist as any of the painters in her books."

"I believe you. But this new one's got me puzzled. I don't know what she's doing with it. Why all the little girls, or almost girls, and why does she have me—the rabbit, I mean—in that ditzy, toed-in pose, looking at the viewer as if I were an intellectual waiting for someone to say something intelligent to me?"

By that time, they had reached the stream. "Look in," Kitty Boy suggested, "and tell me what you see."

Rabbit did. "It just looks wavy, with a fuzzy shape behind and some rocks at the bottom."

"Wait a bit until the waves calm down and focus your eyes on the *surface.* Look at what reflects back."

Rabbit waited, tapping his foot impatiently.

"Hey!" he exclaimed, "it's a rabbit!"

"That's you," Kitty Boy explained.

"That's *me?* Really? I thought you said you saw a handsome cat in there?"

"Yes." Again, Kitty Boy smiled.

"That's strange. I see a really handsome rabbit in there!"

Then Kitty Boy laughed out loud. He laughed until he fell back into the grass, where he rolled around enjoying himself. Rabbit looked at him, perplexed.

"That's you!" Kitty Boy explained.

"So let me get this straight: I look in the water and see me, and you look in the water and see: you! You dog, you. So that's how it works."

Kitty Boy laughed again and continued rolling around in the grass.

"But the painting: that I still don't get," Rabbit said. "All the children just outlined in white, and the draperies, and the snake-tails, and the colorful butterflies—she seems to like those, too. I just don't understand how it all fits together."

"Let's go back and look again. She doesn't mind if we sit on the sill and look in. Maybe we can figure it out," Kitty Boy suggested. "But just a minute: I want to get a drink of water first."

"Don't fall in!" Rabbit warned. "Then you'll be looking out of the water instead of looking in."

"Kind of like you in the painting," Kitty Boy said provocatively.

Rabbit needed some time to think about that one.

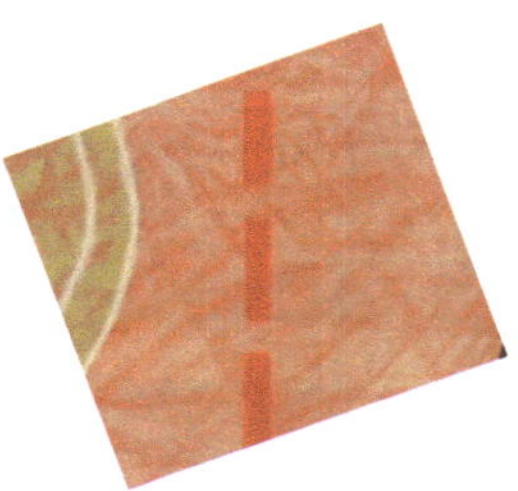

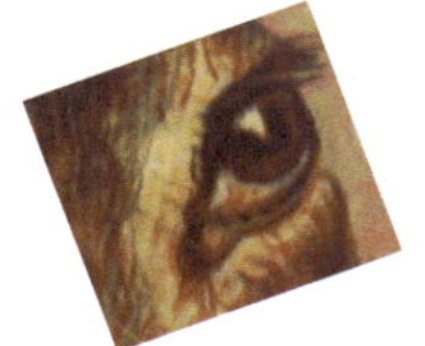

[13]

Mettre Monet en Abime

"Guess what I've been doing," Rabbit said.

He and Kitty Boy were sitting on a large stone next to the stream at the end of the field watching the water flow by.

"Golf," Kitty Boy guessed.

"Golf? Why would I do that?"

"I don't know. The way you said *guess* made me think it must be something pretty odd, and golf came to mind."

"Hmph. So you looked deep into my mind, and you thought you found *golf*?"

"Sorry if I chose poorly. Please tell me what you've been doing, besides sitting here with me on a rock watching the water flow by."

"Well, I guess it's sort of like that, in a way. I've been *meditating*."

"Good for you!" Kitty Boy exclaimed. "I've heard that meditation is good for mental, emotional, and physical health."

"Where did you hear that?"

"Oh, everywhere: you'll find practitioners all over the place if you ask around."

Rabbit felt a little crestfallen, since he thought he'd chosen something unusual and interesting.

"But meditation is still unusual and interesting, if you're worrying about that," Kitty Boy assured him.

"Maybe interesting, but not unusual if everyone's doing it," Rabbit said. "Have you been meditating?"

"Cats always meditate in our own way. We watch a butterfly and let our spirits go outside our bodies to follow it in flight. We chase our tails as a reminder of the futility of pointless violence and the unfathomable mystery of being. We sit in the sun and close our eyes and let the energy of the universe wash over us."

"Wow," Rabbit said, "I had no idea. All cats do that?"

"As far as I know. But you can find lots of ways to meditate. You don't have to practice it the way we do."

"That's good! Even if it's a common practice, I can do my own meditation in an unusual way?"

"Absolutely! So how have you been practicing? But you don't have to tell me if you don't want to: some meditators prefer to keep their practices to themselves—part of their internal life, you know."

Rabbit thought about that for a minute, and then he decided to tell.

"I've been imagining myself inside Monet paintings." He was afraid Kitty Boy would tell him that was a terrible idea.

"Wonderful! I couldn't have thought of a better idea than that."

Rabbit felt very pleased. "I was looking through one of The Artist's books, one that I've seen you using before, and I picked out a painting I like: *Bathers at La Grenouillère*." Rabbit had a flair for French pronunciation. "Then I found a cool, comfortable spot where I could sit by myself, and I crossed my legs, and I imagined I was an Indian mystic, and I sat there on the dock in the painting and, after the bathers had gone, I cleared my mind and watched the water."

"That is a little bit like what we're doing now."

"Except that I'm not by myself or imagining myself sitting on the dock or to be an Indian mystic."

"Did it work?"

"Did what work?"

"Your meditation technique."

"I'm not sure. I don't know what it's supposed to do."

"Did you feel relaxed, at peace with yourself and the world, free of the bonds of life and body?"

"Now that you say it that way, yes, I think it worked."

"Splendid!"

"But is it all right if we meditate together sometimes, like we were just doing here on the rock?"

"Of course: practitioners do that often—sometimes they meditate with one friend, sometimes with many, even a hundred."

"Let's just stick with us two for a while."

"I couldn't agree more," Kitty Boy said. Then he closed his eyes and spoke: "Ommm."

Through Dr. Caligari's Cabinet

Rabbit was sleeping in the house. He felt subconsciously that he should wake up, and he opened one eye to look around. Kitty Boy was sitting there looking at him.

"Do you ever feel like life is a phantasmagoria of fugue states, genetically driven archetypes, contorted dreamscapes, and kaleidoscopic neurotransmissions mediated by a dimly oppressive superego?" Kitty Boy asked.

Rabbit yawned. "No," he said. "Do you?"

"No."

"Then why did you ask me that?"

"The people," Kitty Boy said, "sometimes they say things like that. I thought you might have some answers for them. You know: from your recent meditations."

"Should I be meditating about things like that? I thought I was supposed to clear my mind and free myself from the limitations of thought, desire, and perception."

"You're right. I've heard, though, that sometimes meditation can lead us to revelations about truths for life and spirituality."

"I haven't found any of those yet," Rabbit said. "That seems more like a human problem than a rabbit problem. We don't really go in for Existentialism."

"I guess I wondered because you've been looking more human lately," Kitty Boy intimated.

"I have? Human? Oh, that could be awful! What do I look like?"

"Not always, but sometimes you look like a tall, thin man wearing a turtleneck shirt. You look like you're trying to walk away from someone or something that's trying to control you."

"Do I have a little cloud following me around that seems to be raining just on me?"

"You do! Right out of *Li'l Abner*."

"Yes, I saw that in a dream." Rabbit was beginning to feel afraid and to wonder what he should do.

"But you still have your ears and that irrepressible Rabbit spirit!" Kitty Boy said. "And you have help from outside forces."

"Who are they?" Rabbit asked.

"Ganesha!"

"Who's that?"

"A powerful Indian god who helps those in trouble, giving them guidance and advice: I saw him myself: he's playing the flute and piping encouragement through his trunk right into your ear."

"I'd feel better if you were there, too."

"I am!" Kitty Boy assured his friend. "I'm coming to help in the form of a red bird, diving right toward you to drive away your problems.”

“Thank you! But what advice is Ganesha sending me?”

“I don’t know that. His thoughts seem to be blank. I think it may be just feelings of confidence and friendship and good will. He looks happy enough. Maybe you should be, too.”

Rabbit felt that Kitty Boy always tried to give him the best advice possible, though he didn’t always understand what his friend had to say. He closed his eyes for a moment to think about it. Images that had been swirling in his thoughts faded away, his mind became calm, and he could feel the fuzzy warmth of his favorite cushion beneath him.

He woke.

Kitty Boy was lying on the couch sleeping. Rabbit could see his stomach rise and fall gently as he slept placidly.

I must have been dreaming, Rabbit thought. That was an odd one. But then he realized that having friends come to him in a dream with advice and reassurance was a pretty powerful gift.

He got up to go outside, but first he checked on Kitty Boy. His sleeping friend seemed to be smiling.

Assisted Living

"The ears are nice," Rabbit said.

And the hair's very pretty," Kitty Boy added.

"Otherwise," Rabbit decided, "I don't get it."

"The colors work well together, and the hat has an elegant eighteenth-century *panache* about it."

"The eyes are really scary," Rabbit said.

"Only because of the way The Artist has caught them in the face. Otherwise, they would be pretty, too."

"Let's face it," Rabbit said. "We just don't understand it."

Kitty Boy nodded agreement.

Rabbit and Kitty Boy were standing in The Artist's studio looking at a painting she had just finished. They had both noticed that when she got up to leave, she was crying.

"Why would she paint something that would make her so sad?" Rabbit asked. "Isn't art supposed to make us feel better about life and the world?"

"Ah, maybe you've got something there. What if we think of it this way? Sometimes art makes us feel better, but sometimes it aims to shock us about something painful or sad or troubling or wrong, something that we need to pay attention to but that we've been trying very hard not to think about." Kitty Boy was thinking out loud, and following his thought, he wasn't sure if he'd actually spoken it plainly or not. He waited to see if Rabbit would respond. When he didn't for a minute or two, Kitty Boy tried again, making sure this time to speak clearly.

"Look at all the beautiful individual parts of the painting: colors, brush strokes, composition, emotion. And yet the painting as a *gestalt* remains terrifying. It brings the viewer into the process of metamorphosis, even metempsychosis: our spirits enter into the figure in the painting with compassion and sorrow at her sense of change and loss even amidst conditions of plenty. It draws us toward an epic spiritual catharsis as we confront the tragic fragility of life and love bound in time. We experience individual moments of aesthetic satisfaction, but the whole of any individual's experiences remains transient, sentient but frighteningly fleeting."

"That's exactly what I wanted to say," Rabbit said. "Thank you for putting it so clearly."

"Do you feel better about the painting now?" Kitty Boy asked.

"Not really. Do you?"

"No. But maybe we're not supposed to. Maybe I was wrong about the catharsis. But then again, maybe that's why she painted it: she needed the catharsis herself, and she hoped that the viewer would get the point and experience it, too."

"What's *catharsis*?" Rabbit asked.

"A cleansing of built-up physical or emotional tension so that the audience can return to a state of healthy balance, prepared actively to re-engage with life."

"Say it more plainly, please."

"It's when you feel all clogged up and troubled, and you reach a moment where you let go, and the feeling of discomfort and constriction drops away from you, and you can relax again. It's like when you . . .

"Poo," Rabbit said.

"What?"

"Like when you poo."

"I was going to say," Kitty Boy said, "like when you *laugh*. You're feeling tense and sad, and someone tells a joke, and you laugh, and you feel better."

"Oh. Isn't it sort of the same thing? You said *healthy*, so it can work like a medicine, like munching on some grass to help you . . ."

"We're talking art here, not medicine," Kitty Boy said.

"I see," Rabbit said. He was pretty sure that Kitty Boy was just being stuffy—he gets that way sometimes when he talks about art, Rabbit thought.

"Let's go outside, okay?" Kitty Boy said. "I feel like I need to nibble on some grass."

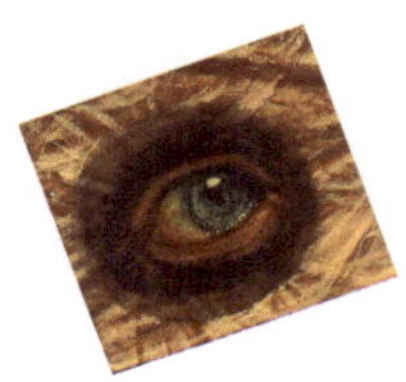

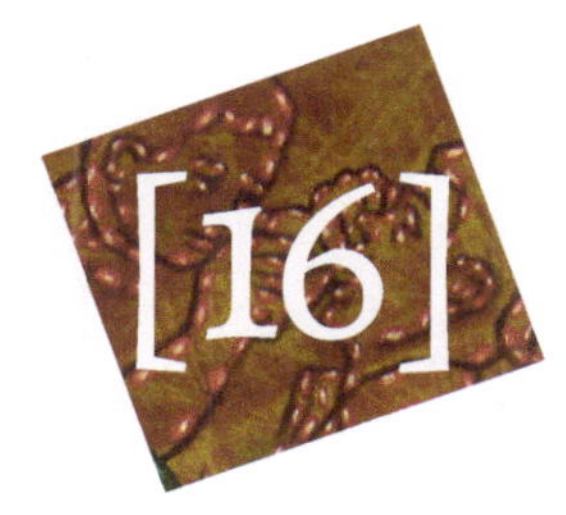

Hank's Rebirth Dilemma

"THIS ONE LOOKS EVEN MORE COMPLICATED THAN THE LAST ONE," Rabbit said.

"It sure does," Kitty Boy agreed, looking over The Artist's new painting. "Less painful, though—except for the cat near the bottom. Why would she paint that?"

"I saw that. But look: he's smiling. So maybe he wasn't well, but he's getting better."

"That's promising."

"Then there's a skinny rabbit in a ball gown."

"Holding a flower, yes. But there's that enormous egg: it must mean something important—maybe some sort of subliminal message."

"It's pretty with that fancy garland, but she looked just as sad this time as she did after the last painting, maybe even worse. Why does she keep doing that to herself? And why does she do it to us? She knows we come in to look at the paintings when she's finished. Can't she just paint something happy?"

"She's not painting them for us. She makes art for a human audience, and they have bigger problems than we do."

"That's because they *make* bigger problems than we do."

Kitty Boy knew Rabbit was right about that, but he didn't think he'd better say anything more about it. He feared that whatever he might say would cause Rabbit to have more nightmares.

"What does the title mean?" Rabbit asked.

"Looks like she's having doubts about someone getting reborn," Kitty Boy answered. "She thinks somebody will come back as an egg."

"Who?"

"Must be *Hank*: someone very important to her. See all the *h*'s?"

"Come back from where?"

"Ah," Kitty Boy said, "one of the great mysteries of life."

"Oh." Anybody who knew about the mysteries of life always impressed Rabbit, because he seldom understood them. He preferred stories of knights and dragons, though he thought they were probably less important. "What are all those other creatures doing in there?"

Kitty Boy was trying not to look too closely: the last painting had given *him* nightmares. But for Rabbit's sake he decided to dive in. "There's a sort-of blue bird of happiness, and another Ganesha, promising new beginnings; there's a dandy tipping his top hat, a laughing doggy-Buddha, a large Puritan rabbit, some butterflies, and a—what's that at the top?—looks like a dentist!—all stitched together."

"What's a dentist?" Rabbit asked.

Kitty Boy found himself feeling very depressed. Dentists reminded him of mortality.

"Humans have them. They work on your teeth. Sometimes cats have to go see them, too."

"Maybe he's a happy dentist," Rabbit said. "Look, everyone else in the painting looks happy, too. Maybe the painting says you have all sorts of choices about what you can be. The egg could be anything: we just have to wait for it to hatch. What fun to see what it will become!"

Kitty Boy sighed. "Thank you, my dear friend: I believe you've got it. I'd missed that entirely." He patted Rabbit on the back. "Say, I'll treat you to lunch today. The sun's come out, and we can talk a long walk out in the field. When we come back, I'll try to get you some of that bubble-water you've been wanting to taste. I know where The Artist keeps it in the refrigerator."

"Ah, that sounds lovely. You are as fine a friend as a rabbit could ask for. But let me make sure about this: today I got the painting, right? I understood it before you did?"

"I believe you did," Kitty Boy said, "and I'm glad for it."

Rabbit glowed with pleasure and began to rub his stomach, thinking about lunch. "Not sure why," Rabbit said, "but I have a taste for an ice-cream cone."

Kitty Boy thought Rabbit had put a more positive spin on the meaning of the painting than he probably should, but he decided that was a very good turn of events indeed. He felt very happy to have his friend, and he decided to say a gentle, encouraging word or two to The Artist when they saw her at suppertime.

Cable or Dish?

"LET'S GO ADVENTURING!" KITTY BOY SAID one morning.

"I'd love to," Rabbit said, "but it's still snowing. I went out last night, and my feet are still freezing." Rabbit hadn't even taken off the scarf he'd tied around his neck the night before to try to stay warm.

"Oh, that's no good. Hey, I have an idea: let's explore in the world of electronics!"

"You mean that store where the people go when they want to buy a tv or a phone or an iPad? That won't work: we'd still have to go outside to get there."

"No, I mean let's dive right into the electronic matrix. We can go surfing on electronic waves! It'll be fun."

Rabbit still didn't understand what Kitty Boy was suggesting, and he wasn't sure he liked the idea. "That doesn't sound fun to me at all."

"It may feel a little scary at first, but we've gone scarier places than that."

"Do you know anyone else who has done it?"

"I saw it in a movie once." Kitty Boy realized that wasn't an especially convincing reason, since all sorts of creatures did all sorts of stupid things in movies all the time.

"How will we get back out again?"

Kitty Boy hadn't thought about that yet. "I'm assuming that if we can get in, we can get back out." He knew that wasn't any more convincing than movies.

"I've heard that people get stuck inside their electronics for hours, even days at time," Rabbit said. "They get addicted, and they can forget even to wash or to eat."

"Forget to eat! That's terrible!" Kitty Boy said. He was beginning to doubt his idea. But then he felt an unexpected rush of boldness. "I'll try it first. Look: I know how to turn on The Artist's iPad. I'll just stick my paw in and see what happens."

"I'll hold on to your leg," Rabbit suggested, "so if anything bad happens, I can pull you right out again."

"That's very brave of you—thank you! Let's go find out what's going on inside those things."

The device was lying on the floor next to some books. Kitty Boy touched the power button with his paw, and lights on the iPad popped on. He waited for a minute, smiled at Rabbit, and thrust his paw into the electronic matrix.

Rabbit just had time to catch Kitty Boy's leg, but it didn't help: Kitty Boy slipped out of his grasp and fell head-after-paw right through the surface of the device into the electronic world.

"What do I do now! My friend is gone, maybe stuck in the electronic world. I have to do something!" Rabbit gathered his courage and prepared to swan-dive straight into the little computer, following

Kitty Boy. But before he could dive for himself, some power grabbed his scarf and tugged him right through the surface into an electrical maelstrom.

The first thing Rabbit noticed was that he felt odd: unstable, like his whole body was vibrating. He felt as if he had spun around a couple times, fallen rapidly, and then landed softly, but he couldn't tell what he'd landed on. His skin tingled, and his fur stood up on end.

He noticed a dish full of water in front of him, and suddenly he felt very thirsty, so he took a drink. The water tasted fine, except that it was full of bubbles, and they made him burp.

"You made it! What do you think?" a voice said to him. But all Rabbit saw was a red butterfly bouncing around just a little above him.

"Think about what?" Rabbit asked. "The water? It's fine, but the bubbles made me burp. Excuse me."

"No, I meant about the place: the electronic world. We're inside it!" the butterfly said.

"Yes, we are. But who are you, and where did Kitty Boy go?"

"Don't you recognize me? I'm right here!"

"Kitty Boy? You've turned into a butterfly? Oh, my, what will I do?"

"Anything you want. You can turn into a butterfly, too, if you'd like, or anything else that comes to mind. Are you sure the water is safe to drink?"

"I have no idea. I just felt thirsty. Are you sure you're Kitty Boy?"

"I was. I think I still am. Let's explore. Where would you like to go?"

"Home: I want to go back home, back to our old world. This one's for, well, butterflies."

"Back home already?"

"Yes."

"Okay. Grab onto my feet, and I'll try to pull us out. No, not the wings—grab my feet. That's it!"

With a great burst of Kitty Boy's wings, Rabbit felt himself pulled upwards. He saw all sorts of strange images swirling around like they were inside a tornado. And then, suddenly, he felt himself pulled through the screen of the iPad back into the house where they had started.

"You can let go of my feet now," Kitty Boy said. "We're home safe. Did you enjoy our adventure?"

"Well, now that we're home and I can think about it, it wasn't so bad. Who'd have thought the bubble water would make me burp like that?"

"Are you feeling all right?"

"Funny, but I feel kind of reborn. You know, like I was lost, but now I'm found again, back home and safe. Did you see all those images as we flew out? I saw shapes and draperies and some kind, gentle faces looking down at a baby. I'm glad we went, but I don't think I want to go back soon. How did you become a butterfly?"

"I don't know. It just seemed like the right thing to do. Now that we've been there, I think we'll always have a little of the electronic world left inside us."

"Hmph," Rabbit muttered. He wasn't sure if that was a good idea or not. He still felt a little of the tingling on his skin: it made him feel alive, but unsettled.

Four Rabbits of the A-Pear-Calypse

"Ever since we got back from the electronic world, I've been having nightmares again, no matter how much I meditate," Rabbit said one evening.

He and Kitty Boy were sitting by a window looking out at a clear sky with a full moon.

"Do you wish we hadn't gone?" Kitty Boy asked.

"No, but now I have all sorts of strange images buzzing around in my head, and I'm not sure what to think of them."

"Tell me. Wait just a minute: I want to get my beret first. I always feel more ready to interpret dreams when I'm wearing it." Kitty Boy dashed off, but he returned in no time sporting his favorite hat. He sat down and said, "Whenever you're ready, my friend."

"Well, the one from last night was particularly troubling."

"Please don't feel like you have to tell about it if you don't want to."

"Four rabbits all flying together like an attack squadron . . . You should have seen their faces: fixed, angry, or maybe resolute, grim and violent. They were attacking something that stood before them, dangerous and ready, and the world around them was spiraling out of control."

"Terrifying!"

"Yes, but here's the strange part: the rabbits all carried pears on their backs."

"Pairs of what?" Kitty Boy asked, wanting to be as clear as possible about what Rabbit had seen.

"Not *pairs*, like two things, but *pears*, like the fruit."

"Oh, sorry: it's a homonym."

"No, it was *pears*. What's a homonym?"

"Words that sound alike. I've got it now: four grim-faced looking rabbits flying to attack an enemy with fruit on their backs."

"Not just any old fruit: *pears*."

"Why did they have pears, do you think?"

"I have no idea."

"What sort of creature were they attacking?"

"I don't know that either. Someone who had done something really bad."

"What made you think that? Are you sure the rabbits were the good guys?"

Rabbit gave Kitty Boy a look that was as close as he could get to scorn. "Of course, they were the good guys. They were *rabbits*."

"I know you're a good guy, Rabbit: you're my dear friend. But not everyone likes rabbits."

"They don't? Who doesn't, and why not?"

"Some people get mad at rabbits for tearing up their gardens or chewing on their plants and trees and ruining them."

"We don't do that on purpose. We're just looking for food. If we get food, we don't do that at all. Certainly, you don't think . . ."

"Of course I don't. I'm your friend, and I understand." Kind of like me and mice, he thought. Kitty Boy wished he hadn't taken the conversation in that direction, so he changed his approach. "So the rabbits were attacking something or someone bad. Whoever that was may have attacked the rabbits, and so the rabbits were fighting back, or they may have done something bad to someone else, and the rabbits were attacking to avenge the victims. Or maybe the bad creatures had just got so bad that the rabbits needed to make a point to convince them not to be bad anymore. So they went to drop pears on them like bombs."

"What good would that do?"

"Better than dropping bombs, which make all sorts of mess. As far as it goes, have you ever been hit by a pear?"

"No."

"If a rabbit dropped it with pinpoint accuracy from high above, it would hurt—a lot."

"Good. Whoever that was must have deserved it. It might bring an end to many kinds of evil."

"Did the dream make you feel sad or scared or righteous or something else?"

"At first it made me scared, but now that we talk about it, I feel like out of a sense of honor I should go drop a pear on someone bad. That would show them."

"It certainly would. But maybe we should go get a snack first."

"That's a good idea: I thought I noticed a savory smell coming from the kitchen. Save the pears if you find any."

Unveiling Celaya's Veil

"WHAT ARE YOU READING?" Kitty Boy asked Rabbit.

He found his friend crouched next to one of The Artist's books next to the bookshelves. Kitty Boy was heading there himself, driven, as his friend was, by a stormy day. The rain poured down so hard that it overran the gutters and fell thick and silvery as tinsel on a Christmas tree.

"I'm not reading," Rabbit replied. "I'm looking at the pictures. It's a book of Re-nai—ssance art."

"What do you see?"

"Almost no cats, and no rabbits at all."

"None?"

"Not a one, at least so far. But lots and lots of Madonna and Child: Madonna and Child, Madonna and Child, Madonna and Child—I think everybody painted the Madonna and Child. Why didn't anyone paint rabbits?"

"The Renaissance was about renewed interest in the human

form, in Classical ideas of proportion, the rediscovery of visual perspective, a refocusing of vision from the heavens to the horizon and the human quest to span the world."

"Why did they care so much about humans?"

"Because they were humans."

"But what about us? Didn't they like us at all?" Rabbit felt not only confused, but miffed.

"They just didn't think about us as very important. We were pretty far down on the Great Chain of Being. They got more and more interested in the human figure in all its glory."

"Not just the human figure: the same human figures. Madonna and Child over and over again. Look."

Rabbit turned a few pages to show Kitty Boy the paintings.

"You're right," Kitty Boy observed. "They all seem to treat the same subject—that's probably what they studied in school. But look at the difference in the faces, in their dimensions and expressions, in the backgrounds and colors. Each one *feels* slightly different. They must have thought of it as expressing their religious zeal as well as their artistic talent. Or maybe that's just what everyone else asked them to paint."

"Look here," Rabbit said, "at this other book." He pulled down another from a shelf. "I looked at this one last week. I try to look at one new book each week to improve my knowledge."

"Good for you!" Kitty Boy responded, encouragingly. "Education improves all of us, and I appreciate your commitment."

"Thank you. Now look at the pictures in this book." Rabbit opened the book and turned the pages right past the introduction and into many pages of colored plates. "See how different it all looks?"

Modernism and Abstraction," Kitty Boy said, "that's the title. No wonder the pictures look so different: in *that* time everybody was reacting against all the painting that had come before."

"No need to explain that to me," Rabbit said. "If I'd had to paint copy after copy of Madonna and Child, I'd have made a whole bunch of paintings like these, and I'd have left them all over town for everyone to see. I'd have painted all sorts of shapes and colors, and I'd have thrown in hair and stones and beeswax, and maybe on top of that I would have sprayed some . . ."

"Oh, don't say that!" Even Kitty Boy thought Rabbit was going too far.

"Well, after painting the same thing for hundreds of years wouldn't you just want to break out with something adventurous and different and funny and outrageous?"

Kitty Boy wasn't sure if he would do that, but he could understand why Rabbit would want to. "I can understand why you'd say that," he said.

"I have this idea," Rabbit said, "and I think I'll try to tell The Artist about it. Maybe she'll like it. You have a big, royal-purple background, and in the middle you have one of these Re-nai-ssance babies, and around him you have a bunch of heads from the other babies . . ."

"Oh, that's terrible!"

"No, just listen for a minute. But, see, one of the heads isn't a head at all, but a pumpkin right out of the pumpkin patch, and it has this totally surprised and scared look at its face, because the child is sending out a radar and calling toward him a great big ghost rabbit that's darting down toward him from the sky, because unlike the other people around he likes rabbits, too—he likes everyone. And the other heads represent everyone else looking on as the rabbit comes down when the baby calls to help him wipe out human self-obsession. And it would have lots and lots of wrinkles and veils. Wouldn't that make a great painting?"

"It might," Kitty Boy admitted. "It just might." He smiled.

"It wouldn't just be Modern or Abstract like this book, it would be . . . would be . . . *post*-Modern, like you told me before, and *post*-Abstract. Wouldn't that be fun? Maybe someone would take it and put it in a book and our artist would be famous, too."

"Let's tell her," Kitty Boy said. "She's never afraid to try new ideas."

And they did.

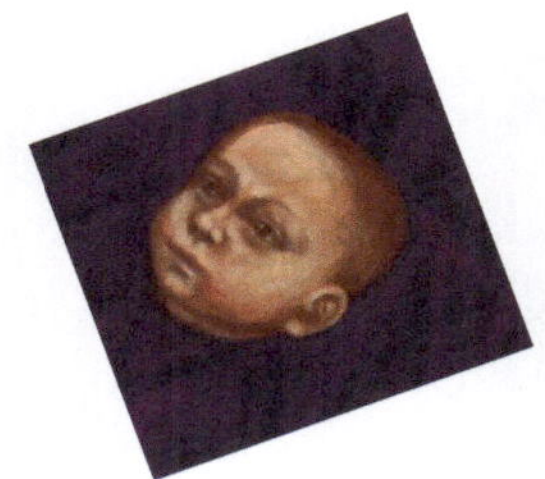

[20]

Targeting Tuyman's Rabbit

"DIDN'T YOU SEE THE NEW PAINTING? Why would she want to target me?" Rabbit asked, afraid. "I've always been nice, and she's always been nice to me, and I've never taken anything from her garden except maybe a few carrots and some flowers and herbs, but she never said that made her mad. I'm so upset."

Kitty Boy was following Rabbit across the field in back of the house. He was afraid his friend was going to run away. Rabbit was walking on his hind legs with his front paws covering his face. Kitty Boy had never seen him so worried.

"Look," Kitty Boy said, "that's not even you in the painting. The Artist says it's *Tuyman*'s rabbit: he's the one who first painted it, and she borrowed it from him."

"Maybe it's a case of displaced aggression."

"Why do you think it's aggression at all?"

"Did you see the big target-shape?"

"Yes."

"The middle of the target falls right where my eye should be. And there's a hummingbird pecking at my eye with its beak! That seems pretty aggressive to me!" Rabbit flopped down and began to cry. "What did I do that was so bad?"

"Did you notice the shape in the center of the target?"

"It looks like lips. What sense does that make?"

"You're the one who turned her on to postmodernism with your Renaissance-baby heads."

"Oh: do you think that's why she got angry?" Rabbit sniffed.

"I don't think she's angry at all. Listen: the hummingbird isn't attacking anyone. It looks to be reaching down to kiss the lips. It's a happy image, a vision of love and connection."

"But that's where my *eye* should be!"

"It's not you!" Kitty Boy was adamant. "It's a white rabbit, and you're not a white rabbit, and it's Tuyman's rabbit, not *the Rabbit*, you. She's making up for what the Renaissance artists left out. And it's not even an eye: it's a mouth, like in those Renaissance metaphysical poems. And the bird certainly isn't pecking. In fact, I think it's placing a drop of healing nectar in the rabbit's mouth so that it will stop feeling sad and see the world more hopefully. That's the reason for *target* in the title, so she can help heal all of the rabbits in the world and make everyone feel special: an awfully nice way to end a series of paintings."

"Do you really think so?" Rabbit asked.

"Yes, I do."

"You'll always be my best friend, Kitty Boy," Rabbit said, smiling.

"Thank you. I'm glad for that, and you'll be my best friend, too. Are you feeling better yet?" Kitty Boy asked.

"A little."

"How about we go adventuring," Kitty Boy suggested.

"That sounds nice. Where would you like to go?"

"How about India? We haven't been there for a while. We could look for tigers and pashas and poets and ask them to tell us stories."

"That sounds nice. But can we go to Paris first, a nice little café along the Seine? I could really use a big salad with lots of greens to help me feel better." Rabbit allowed himself one more little sniffle.

"Absolutely," Kitty Boy said, starting to feel hungry, too.

And off they went.

KRISTY DEETZ is a Professor in the Art Discipline at the University of Wisconsin—Green Bay. Her extensive exhibition record includes national and international venues and her paintings have been featured in a number of textbooks and magazines. She frequently gives workshops and serves as a visiting artist at venues including Haystack, Oxbow, Penland, and Arrowmont. UWGB awarded her the 2011 Founders Award for Excellence in Scholarship and she received SECAC's 2016 Award for Excellence in Teaching. In 2018, she served as Erasmus Visiting Lecturer at the University of Kassel, Germany, and as artist-in-residence at The Burren College of Art in Ireland.

EDWARD S. LOUIS (pen name for E. L. Risden, Professor of English, St. Norbert College) lives, teaches, and writes in Wisconsin. His hobbies include daily practice of tai chi chuan and Mediterranean cooking. Previous books include *The Monster Specialist* (2014), *Odysseus on the Rhine* (2005), *White Shoes* (2017), *The Streets of Harmon Falls* (2016). Louis has recently completed a new novel, *Between Such Distant Shores*, and a collection of short stories, *A Brief History of Friendship*. Kristy and Ed have a house lion, Bingley, who keeps them both in line.